International acclaim for
Kate Jennings's **SNAKE**

"*Snake* can be read in a single sitting. In fact, this is the ideal way to absorb Ms. Jennings's stunning narrative. . . . Clearly the work of a powerful imagination."
— Carol Shields, *New York Times Book Review*

"How often do you find a book that seizes you and doesn't let go until it has finished its assault? *Snake* does that, quite painfully and beautifully. . . . Shivers of suspense flow over the reader of this tale. . . . The novel races the reader to its tragic climax."
— Evelyn Juers, *Australian Book Review*

"Kate Jennings's style is as spare and compelling as the landscape of her native country. The reader can feel the heat and smell the disillusionment of this Australian rural scene, captured in breathtaking detail."
— Jill Ker Conway

"What astonishment, stimulation, refreshment, enjoyment is to be found in this short novel."
— Elizabeth Riddell, *The Bulletin* (Sydney)

"This snake of a novel is lethal and fast-moving. . . . Domestic dystopia has rarely been distilled into such concentrated literary form."
— *Publishers Weekly*

"Immensely readable. . . . What could be a long family saga is told within a very short space, and the landscape, the characters, the events are at their most succinct and vivid. . . . A novel that simmers with energy, passion, and thoroughly unresolved tensions."

— Debra Adelaide, *Sydney Morning Herald*

"Irresistibly good. . . . *Snake* is large with the difficulty of our being, and with Kate Jennings's intelligence and art. She has the power, and the unsparing humanity, to show us our inward selves and to set our dreams and our blunders in the great, indifferent world. Her writing obliges us to understand and to grow."

— Shirley Hazzard

"*Snake* is a slender book, a mere 157 pages, and those with generous margins, but in them is condensed a much longer novel's strength, insight, charm, and emotion."

— Bryant Urstadt, *Valley Advocate* (Northampton, MA)

"A natural for the Booker short-list. . . . The chapters in *Snake* resemble a string of prose poems. Few are longer than a short paragraph, yet each is perfectly placed to forward a narrative of pure anguish."

— Les Murray, *Times Literary Supplement* (London)

"The chapters in *Snake* are short, vivid bursts of imagery, anecdote, insight. . . . You can easily read the entire book in one sitting — and only upon standing be struck by how much pity and terror you've consumed."

— Michelle Huneven, *Los Angeles Times Book Review*

"The claustrophobia of [Irene and Rex's] situation, which leads with seeming inevitability to tragedy, is brilliantly captured in the terse, poem-like chapters that Jennings uses to tell her story. *Snake* is a book that will come to be regarded as a classic account of the realities of Australian rural life."

— Jamie Grant, *People* (Australian edition)

"*Snake* is a poet's novel, but without any poetic language. Instead it is written in a lean muscular prose and, which was a very clever stratagem, tells a long and complicated family history in prose poem thimblefuls. It works brilliantly. . . . The primary achievement of *Snake* is the way in which it uses words to convey the precise little hell of emotional wordlessness."

— Andrew Field, *Courier-Mail* (Brisbane)

"Beautifully written, exquisitely painful, insidiously memorable."

— Katharine England, *Adelaide Advertiser*

SNAKE

ALSO BY KATE JENNINGS

POETRY
Come to Me My Melancholy Baby
Mother I'm Rooted (editor)
Cats, Dogs & Pitchforks

STORIES
Women Falling Down in the Street

ESSAYS
Save Me, Joe Louis
Bad Manners

S N A K E

Kate Jennings

BACK BAY BOOKS

LITTLE, BROWN AND COMPANY
Boston   New York   London

Originally published in hardcover by The Ecco Press, 1997

First Back Bay paperback edition, 1998

Reprinted by arrangement with The Ecco Press

Library of Congress Cataloging-in-Publication Data
Jennings, Kate
    Snake/Kate Jennings.—1st Ecco ed.
      p.   cm.
    ISBN 0-88001-538-1 (hc) 0-316-91258-1 (pb)
    I. Title.
PR9619.3.J44S65   1997
823—dc20   94-41698

10   9   8   7   6   5   4   3   2   1

MV-NY

Published simultaneously in Canada by Little, Brown & Company (Canada) Limited

Printed in the United States of America

When the dog at morning
Whines upon the frost
I shall be in another place.
Lost, lost, lost.

ELIZABETH RIDDELL

SNAKE

PART ONE

1

Poor Devil

Everybody likes you. A good man. Decent. But disappointed. Who wouldn't be? That wife. Those children.

Your wife. You love and cherish her. You like to watch her unobserved, through a window, across a road or a paddock, as if you were a stranger and knew nothing about her. You admire her springy hair, slow smile, muscled legs, confident bearing. If this woman were your wife, your chest would swell with pride.

She is your wife, she despises you. The coldness, the forbearing looks, the sarcastic asides, they are constant. She emasculates you with the sure blade of her contempt. The whirring of the whetstone wheel, the strident whine of steel being held to it, that is the background noise to the nightmare of your days.

.

She passes on the loathing she feels for you to the children, solemnly, as if it were an heirloom. They grow up ignoring you. They are not your children; they are hers, with her hopes, virtues, faults. When they were born, you stood over their cots and wished for them sturdy bodies, strong bones, and a sense of fairness. Now you look at them and think, *foreigners.*

Every reason to be disappointed, although that word implies expectations, and you never had many of them.

2

Rex Redux

You grew up on a farm, a thousand acres of chalky soil, a rainfall to break the strongest spirit. The days always began with your father, shoulders hunched against the half-light of dawn, trekking across the yard, past the clothesline, to the rainfall gauge. Any kind of precipitation, even a heavy dew, was marked with ceremony on the calendar that hung on the back of the kitchen door.

You were a taciturn child, skinny, with freckles, and you looked at people with a shy, sideways squint. You had a younger brother who was your opposite: a plump bully. One day your brother—he was ten, you were twelve—whacked his pony with a piece of wire, and the beast bucked, for the moment made as vicious as her master. As your brother fell, his boot snagged in the stirrup, and he was jounced against hard ground from the sheep shed to the house.

He didn't scream; he squealed. You all heard him. Who knew a human could produce a noise like that? By the time the horse reached the house, your brother was unconscious. The pony stood quietly, flicking her tail, spittle looping from her mouth, ignoring the inert boy with the bloodied head and arms that dangled from the saddle on her back.

Broke every bone in his body, your parents told neighbors when they came to commiserate. As with all disasters—hailstorms, foot-and-mouth disease, miscarriages—their tone was reverential, boastful even, as if his accident had been an achievement.

They set up a bed in the living room and waited for gangrene to set in, as it must, things always went from bad to worse in their world. Your parents were familiar with gangrene; in a similar makeshift bed in the same room, your grandfather had died piece by piece, the smell of his rotting flesh perfuming the air, a magnolia blooming in hell.

For once, events were in their favor; your brother's wounds healed, his bones knit. His luck was your misfortune. The farm couldn't support two sons, one of you would have to go into the world, and it had to be you, you were fit, capable.

The decision broke your heart. You would have been happy to spend your life in that small wooden house on its stony hill, the sheltering stand of ironbarks, the paddocks spread below, the dams with their chocolate water. You are one of those people who take comfort from the sameness of their surroundings.

It seemed all the more unfair as your brother's brush with death had not humbled him; if anything, he took up his career as a sly tyrant with renewed vigor. They should have called him Rex, not you.

3

Light Doth Seize My Brain

The year of your brother's accident, you stayed home from school to help with the wheat harvest and never went back, which was no loss, or so you thought, only a step toward becoming a man.

Your school was easy to forget: a one-room structure in the middle of nowhere. Bare-bones arithmetic, grammar, spelling. Penmanship exercises. *Little Arthur's History of England.* The teacher was nicknamed Tommy-gun because he tommy-gunned you with his saliva. Sparrow shit on the desk. The harrumphing of ponies hitched to the verandah posts.

You have come to regret keenly your lack of education. You strain your whole being toward knowledge. If you could only concentrate long enough, you would have answers. Answers to what?

That is part of the problem. The questions don't come easily, either.

In your family, nothing beyond the essential was named, no stories told, no future imagined, no god worshipped. Whatever had brought your parents to the present time was best ignored; it was probably only more of the same. They endured by putting one foot in front of the other, not by bending a knee.

People who spoke in consecutive sentences were indulging themselves; they were of the same order as tipplers and gluttons. Remarks beyond those necessary to get things done passed their lips as rarely as cacti have flowers, and were as startling.

Their wordlessness arose from frugality but was also a precaution. To describe the world was to risk admitting the inadmissible: their way of life— tilling a blighted soil under a punishing sun—was intolerable.

4

In the Stream the Shadowy Fish

Midday. The sun presses down. In the dust of the yard, dogs scuffle over a bone crawling with ants. Inside, your parents, your brother, and you are eating lunch. There is no conversation, but the radio is on, tuned to the livestock and grain report. An oilskin tablecloth, pickles, fatty mutton, celery salad, white bread, milky tea.

Presiding over this scene is an elaborately framed photograph of your father. The studio flash has given him a glassy-eyed expression, and he is wearing an ill-fitting Light Brigade uniform: cockaded hat, jodhpur pants, riding whip. After the meal, your mother does the dishes while your father sleeps slack-mouthed on a red-leather chaise placed in the hallway to take advantage of any movement in the air.

5

Grey Dreams

There were winters, of course, with frost that crackled underfoot and wind that blew through the floorboards of the house. Boots were stamped in the morning, bottoms toasted at the fireplace in the evenings, and, on getting into bed, legs bicycled to warm up icy sheets. But the cold was brief, an annoyance; heat was the element that shaped your lives. Good days, ninety degrees, ninety-five, one hundred. Bad days, one hundred and fifteen in the shade. Heat of that order is a brutish master: truth, fact, circumstance, all in one.

You never minded the physical world into which you were born. Drought, dust storms, erosion, this you accepted. What you have always found terrible is the region your heart inhabits, your imagination dwells. It is always dusk in this place; darkness is not far off. It is cool rather than cold. With a hint of damp. You are not aware of the moisture in the air until you touch your cheek and feel it lying lightly there. Over to one side, a tree, not in silhouette, more of a smudge. You stand alone, in the cool, the dampness spreading its invisible film, the blackness advancing.

Of course you are disappointed. How could you not be? But more than that, you are lonely. You are imprisoned in loneliness.

PART TWO

1

Je Suis une Dame!

Billie was noticing how Irene, in her excitement, kept forgetting herself. She'd break into a stride, causing the silk of her wedding dress to pull tight across her thighs. Thus checked, she reverted to smaller, more ladylike steps. The next minute, though, her gait widened, and she was off again, hiking from group to group in her parents' garden, proferring her cheek for kisses, accepting good wishes, queen for the day.

Billie—Wilhelmina at her christening, Billie thereafter—was Irene's bridesmaid and pal from the army. Her eyes skipped over the guests until she located the groom, whose name was Rex. He was chatting with Irene's parents, a handsome fellow with a gentle manner and a modest row of medals pinned to his uniform, and of interest beyond his role as groom, being freshly returned from the Victory March in London. Billie found it easy to understand why Irene had fallen for him. But, poor lamb, he did look bewildered, rather like a schoolboy who'd lost his lunch money.

With the war ended, girls were scrambling for husbands as if they were playing musical chairs, or so it seemed to Billie. And Irene was scrambling harder than most, probably because she had lost face when a fling with a Yank soldier fizzled. The relationship had progressed as far as an engagement ring, and then the young man returned from whence he came—the land of canned ham and chewing gum—and was never heard from again.

Irene's next boyfriend was a Maori, from a company of native New Zealanders. Misalliances were the order of the day, but gossip about that twosome ricocheted around the AWACs barracks like a bullet. Some of the women were of the opinion that Irene had taken up with him deliberately, to shock, but Billie disagreed. Irene acted on impulse, she told them, and didn't give too much thought to things.

These same women said Irene was "fast," and Billie supposed she was: Irene was notorious for breaking the rules, climbing out the window after lights were out, off to a movie or a dance. They said she was a man's woman, and it was true that Irene quickened in the company of the opposite sex; she came alive as water does when invaded by schools of turning fish. Men responded in kind; no need to cajole.

Interestingly, to Billie anyway, whose family was Methodist and practiced what was preached to them, Irene never missed Communion on Sundays. Observing Irene in her native habitat—the big house on Sydney's North Shore, the relatives with the plummy vowels that disguised the heartlessness of their remarks—Billie wondered if Irene's kind weren't born knowing the way to the nearest Anglican church. In her mind's eye, Billie saw the translucent body of an infant kangaroo, eyelids squeezed shut, groping through its mother's fur in the direction of the pouch, and then Irene and her siblings and cousins, similarly reduced, making for St. James.

Billie turned her attention to Irene's parents. They were still engaged in conversation with Rex. Irene's mother was adjusting the spray of orchids she was wearing on her shoulder, and her father was replying to something Rex had said and nodding at guests as they walked by. Her mother was tall and thin and had an ungenerous set to her mouth, in contrast to her father, who was small and round, with a self-effacing air.

"*Mère et père,*" said Billie, showing off her schoolgirl French. Next, she cast around for Daphne, Irene's older sister and the matron of honor. But Daphne had disappeared.

2

Good Lord, Deliver Us

Daphne was at the bottom of the garden, where there was a swing seat with a canvas awning. She was pushing hard with her heels—the seat was fairly rattling with effort!— and deciding that Irene was in for a comeuppance. Rex was a nice enough chap but about as interesting as a month of rainy Sundays. Irene will be bored with him before they arrive at the Blue Mountains guesthouse for their honeymoon.

Daphne based her estimation of Rex on the answer she had received when she questioned him about the Victory March. She had expected a vivid picture of the celebrations—the water cannon and fireworks, the Royal Family—but Rex declined to describe anything, saying he had been marching and the only view he'd had was of the neck of the man in front of him. And, he'd confided, it was a dirty neck. Uncertain how that last observation would be received, he punctuated it with a bleat of nervous laughter.

3

I Will Walk within My House with a Perfect Heart

Irene's mother's dominant emotion on the day of the wedding was relief: Rex was white, Protestant, presentable. With Irene, one never knew. She viewed Irene as a changeling in the nest. From early on her daughter's guile had been a source of dismay. And then the war came, and Irene went—what was the phrase people used?—man-crazy.

Irene's mother was wearing a hat with a veil that superimposed black dots on everything she inspected, which at that moment was Irene, come to a halt by her new husband's side. Irene and Rex were dewy with youth and sensuality. Irene's mother felt one should avert one's head at private intentions made so public.

Like many women of her class, Irene's mother maintained a separate bedroom from her husband; he could make his own arrangements. On the rare occasions she thought about sex, it was to envisage the gully at the bottom of the hill near her house—gloomy, vine-tangled, rank with the smell of still water and furtive animals.

Irene's mother was a punctilious woman. She was like a toy electric train whizzing along its track, under the pass, over a trestle, by the signal box, and back round again. Every night she smoothed on face cream and slipped between starched sheets, where she read a psalm before switching off the light—"I will sing of mercy and judgment: unto thee, O Lord, will I sing" was a favorite—and falling almost immediately asleep. On rising, she flexed her limbs in a series of exercises that never varied. Erect posture and a firm bosom—shopgirls say bustline, we say bosom—were a creed with her.

She gave the impression of being stone-hearted, concerned with her own comfort, the pot of tea stewed for exactly five minutes, shortbread biscuits that were neither moist nor dry, steak-and-kidney pie with a quarter-inch crust, a thimbleful or two of Madeira wine. The best brocade curtains, damask table linen, broadloom carpet, vitreous china fixtures. Yet she'd had her share of sadnesses: twins who had died at birth, a self-sufficient husband, an ambition to enter a profession.

That last item would have come as a shock to anyone who knew her. They would have fallen off their chairs in surprise! Not only that, she knew which profession: she had shown an aptitude for arithmetic when she was young, so she had always thought she would make an excellent engineer. Specifically, Irene's mother wanted to be the sort of engineer who built roads and bridges.

4

One of Nature's Gentlemen

Irene came to a halt by her husband, but her feet did not stay still; they jiggled. Her father saw this and thought, as he often had, she dances to a tune no one else hears. He glanced at his watch, wondering how long it would be before the guests departed and he could disappear into his greenhouse, where there was a *Gloriosa superba* in bloom. He had a passion for the Liliaceae family, which he much preferred to his human one, being the kind of man who recoiled from clamor.

Despite his solitary habits, Irene's father was liked by everyone. Mildness was his chief characteristic, although he was far from being without blemish, having prejudices with prodigious taproots. These prejudices originated in the antimacassar-draped drawing-rooms of his English forebears and concerned, predictably, Asians, Jews, and Catholics. "Good stock" was a phrase he often used, but it was judged a harmless preoccupation, the product of the plantsman in him.

He and his wife regarded Rex's parents—they were there, well scrubbed, liberally talcumed, decked in their Sunday best, unhappily clutching plates with slices of half-eaten wedding cake on them—as being lower down the evolutionary line. Yet they themselves had no books in the house, excepting gardening manuals and Georgette Heyer romances. They had no interest in any of the other arts, either. They had never caught the train to the Town Hall for a concert; their walls were decorated with autumnal-hued prints depicting maidens in Roman costume disporting themselves around wading pools and cows wending their way through bosky English countryside. These were people so certain of their own superiority they need not remark on it; in their complacency, they resembled well-stuffed sofas.

5

The Wind at Your Door

Rex knew Irene's family's opinion of
him. Snobs, he said to himself, the
first time he met them. It hadn't mattered; he was
marrying Irene and not them. But now that the
deed was done, he was filled with foreboding. He
imagined leaving the wedding breakfast, the cake
with its little pillars and artificial flowers and net
bows, the guests chittering like starlings in a tree,
closing the front gate after him with a click, and
walking down the suburban street, past the high
hedges and tennis courts and the houses with their
circular driveways, as if he were Gulliver in Lilliput,
past Parramatta, over the Blue Mountains, coastal
green turning to desiccated brown, until he was far
away, until he was home.

He stifled the urge to cry. He had cried only
once in his adult life, and that was the day he went

to the Royal Sydney Showground to enlist. It was his first time in a city, and he had not known how to do the simplest things, such as purchase a ticket for a bus, and was too proud, too shy, to ask for assistance.

He somehow found his way by foot from Central Station to the showground at Randwick, where he was told to take off his clothes and line up with other enlistees, also naked, to be scrutinized by boot-clicking officers with moustaches that framed mouths that seemed unnaturally small and red-lipped.

Being fastidious in his personal habits—his family never intruded on one another—and never having had communal contact with boys other than his brother, he was humiliated by the order to strip down and stand "in the nuddy." In truth, he found this more shocking than the horrors of war, men split open like pomegranates left on the branch. He was a farm boy and refused to be sentimental; innards were innards, men or sheep.

He went from the showground to his Aunt Em's, to spend the night. She was a spinster who lived at Coogee and worked behind the stocking counter at Anthony Hordern's. He stood on her doormat, under a weak porch light, and before she could say a word of welcome, he began to cry, not silently but with racking sobs, venting his anguish about all that had gone before, all that was in front of him.

Aunt Em was a hard case—as hard as the boiled

lollies she sucked all day long and made her breath smell sickly sweet. In her book, a boy on the verge of manhood had no business with tears. She took in the too-short pant legs, the fresh haircut, the out-of-control Adam's apple, and felt only one emotion: embarrassment.

Rex glanced at Irene. She was glowing with happiness. The sight of her caused his nature—practical, honorable—to assert itself. He put his misgivings aside, hid them under a pile of other thoughts, as if they were shirts without buttons or bills that needed paying. What was done was done. Without being conscious of it, he coughed self-importantly—I am a man, I have a wife—and squirmed inside the jacket of his uniform until it sat better on his shoulders.

6

Oh Such a Hungry Yearning

Irene's father was wrong: the tunes in Irene's head were not her exclusive property. They were known to millions, big band tunes for the most part: insistent trumpets, urgent saxophones, persuasive clarinets. Irene was under the spell of music that was strutting, silky, optimistic, in thrall to smoky-voiced singers and innuendo-laced lyrics. Tommy Dorsey and Benny Goodman, Frank Sinatra and Peggy Lee, they were the snake charmers and Irene the snake.

Billie was closer to being right about Irene than any who toasted her on the occasion of her marriage to Rex: Irene's motives were not complicated or deep. She was only twenty years old, her getting of wisdom had been in the precipitous, snuggle-and-kiss years of World War II. She had only one thought in her head the day of her wedding: *My life is about to begin.*

PART THREE

1

Far-flung Empire

The house was wooden and raised on posts a foot above the ground, and had a verandah on two sides, a pantry off the kitchen, a lean-to laundry, a chip heater in the bathroom, a toilet over a pit out the back. It was not without decorative elements: a fireplace with a mantel in the sitting-room, and in the main bedroom, a set of windows that had pressed glass in three colors—yellow, purple, green—in the upper sashes. The floors were covered with linoleum, except for the bathroom, where the concrete had been left bare.

There was no garden to speak of, unless you counted the stumps of four palm trees, which had been hollowed out, filled with earth, and planted with pigface. The pigface was in bloom the day the newlyweds arrived, its circus colors spilling down the sides.

Irene and Rex walked up the path and stopped at the steps to the verandah. One of the steps hung loose. "I'll have that fixed in a jiffy," said Rex, asserting himself in a voice thick with responsibility.

His tone annoyed Irene. She brushed the feeling away, but it re-formed, hovered, settled, like a mantle of flies on a hot day.

2

The Moral Is the Universal One: "Let Us Irrigate"

The house belonged to Irene's father, as did the farm on which it sat: eight hundred irrigated acres, five hundred miles from the nearest city, nine miles from the nearest town. Rex went as a share farmer, a status he had been brought up to view as ignominious—better to own one acre than manage ten thousand—but he was thankful for the opportunity of a new start.

The fact that it was an irrigation farm helped his decision. No anxious scanning of the skies, no tightening of the gut as the days without rain became months and then years; instead, he would order water from the water bailiff in the same way he bought seed and fertilizer from the stock and station agent.

He felt, too, a connection to the area: his grandfather, forced off his land near the Victorian border by drought, had found work there, hauling sand on a bullock wagon. It seemed to Rex that Irene's family could easily have been his, scraping to make a living, if misfortune had chosen to dog them. Whenever he was told stories to do with success or failure, Rex always intoned with the regularity of a clock striking the hour, "It's the luck of the game."

Because of the war, the farm had been neglected. Channels needed to be cleared of weed, banks recontoured, paddocks graded. Rex thought of his years in the service as a long, tedious round of setting up camp only to pull it down again; in contrast, this work was deeply satisfying. Soon he was flushing the paddocks with water; ibis came, and spoonbill. Rex grew wheat with full, firm ears and grazed wethers with rounded sides.

He took childish pleasure in watching water flow down a freshly delved furrow, filling the depressions, turning clods into islands, enveloping them. Once, he pulled off his thick-soled work boots and scratchy woolen socks, rolled up the pant legs of his overalls, and waded into a half-filled channel. Mud squeezed between his toes; it was not an unpleasant sensation.

His feet were magnified by the rippling water; they were as white as wall plaster and traced with prominent ink-blue veins, in contrast to his face and forearms, which were weathered to a uniform reddish-brown. The world burned, but he was up to his ankles in cold water. If he had been an expressive man, he would have shook his fist at the sun.

3

Who Would Live in a Country Town?

Irene looked down at the baby girl clamped to her nipple, the screwed-up purplish-red face, balled fists, jerking legs, and remembered the cat in the woodpile. She had pulled away a log to reveal a cranny in which a cat was at that moment giving birth to a kitten. The cat was a fine specimen, black and white, with a queenly set of whiskers. Irene crouched down, and before her very eyes, the cat, seemingly without effort, expelled a kitten from her vagina, a tiny thing wrapped in white membrane, the umbilical cord securing it to its mother like a ship to a dock.

What the cat should then have done, after an initial moment of puzzlement at finding an alien object attached to her, was free the kitten from its caul, lick its nose and mouth clean, bite through the cord. But something was wrong with the cat's instincts. Instead of turning maternal, she had become angered. She swatted at the kitten as if it were a mouse, swatted again, and realizing it wasn't about to run away, devoured it. After, she cleaned her whiskers.

"Your baby, ma'am. Pay attention." The baby had come unattached from Irene's nipple and was butting blindly at her chest. It was the ward sister, a small woman with large shoulders. "You must try harder. After all, you can't return your baby to the baby shop." The sister chuckled at her own joke.

"What happens now?" asked Irene of no one in particular. She was on the edge of hysteria.

The sister ignored her. Instead, she came over and peered at the baby. "I think she's had enough," she said, and took the bundle from Irene. "I'll get the nurse to bring you some Ovaltine. That'll settle you."

"Bloody Ovaltine," said Irene, after the sister had disappeared from view. "Bloody baby, bloody everything." She relieved herself of her frustration in low tones, but the woman in the next bed overheard, and soon the whole town knew about Irene's rebellion.

4

Pseudonaja Textilis Textilis

Irene's favorite dish was corned beef and asparagus with white sauce. She bought a slab of cured silverside, trimmed the fat, boiled it for three hours with peppercorns, vinegar, and a bay leaf. As for the asparagus, it grew on the channel banks, pale tips pushing plumply through the loam. If the day was cool, she strapped the baby—they had given her Irene's mother's name but called her Girlie—into a wicker seat on the back of her bicycle and pedaled to a bridge over a fast-running feeder channel.

She leaned the bike against the railing and, with the baby on her hip, threaded her way along the bank, stepping carefully between clumps of sticky paspalum, on the lookout for the telltale bright-green feathery foliage of the asparagus plants but also for snakes, the brown variety: long, fast, deadly.

All you saw of them was the dull glitter of scales or a tail section soundlessly exiting, unless you were unlucky enough to step on one, in which case the snake formed an S-shape with its forebody and, jaws fixed in a hideous rictus, struck repeatedly.

Irene was bumping over a rut in the road when Girlie's heel jammed in the spokes of the bike. Her shoe was wrenched off, the skin of her heel peeled back. Girlie shrieked; Irene felt only irritation. She was pregnant again. It was a boy. She was certain of that.

5

The Genus Iris

Girlie's heel mended, and Boy was born. For a time, Irene was happy. Rex bought her a Hoover twin-tub washing machine, and into it she fed his mud-encrusted overalls. He also bought her a Singer sewing machine, and she bent her head to make clothes for herself and the children, decorating them with zigzag stitching, courtesy of a novel attachment that also made buttonholes.

She learned to bottle fruit. From the orchardists on the other side of Progress, she bought cases of apricots, peaches, pears, and plums, halved and de-stoned the fruit, layered it in jars. Then she added syrup, sealed the jars with rubber rings, clamped on the metal tops, and cooked the fruit on the top of the stove, a vigilant eye on the thermometer. The pantry took on the appearance of a cave heaped with treasure: amber, amethyst, glints of gold. Sometimes Irene went in there for no other reason than to admire her handiwork.

Whenever she could, she gardened. Ahead of her time, she planted natives: banksia, bottlebrush, grevillea, wattle. Following her father's example with lilies, she conceived a plan to cultivate irises in a large square bed, each rivaling the next, as she had seen at the Botanical Gardens in Sydney. Rex dug the bed to her specifications, his rotary hoe belching blue smoke. She sent away to a nursery for rhizomes and planted them in a grid. Beside each one, she placed a stake with the relevant botanical name.

6

Crown'd with Snakes

There was never any one day when Irene took in the details of her life and formulated the thought, I want to be someone else, I want to be somewhere else. Instead, the irritation she felt when Rex offered to fix the step grew in her like an iris rhizome, bulbous and knotted, to be divided and planted elsewhere, time and again.

She hardly understood what was happening. She woke determined to be cheerful, but by the middle of the day some small thing plunged her into a fury. She knitted her lips, pained by everyone and everything, except for her beautiful blue-eyed Boy-o.

Irene's moods filled the house; there was no escaping. Rex was pinned by them to the walls, pushed into corners. Leaving the house did not make it any better; everywhere, sweeping blue sky, an horizon that stretched to the back of beyond, and yet he was suffocating.

Irene could go for days without speaking, sleeping with her back to him, doing her chores with tears in her eyes, biting on her lip, turning so he could only see her profile. Then, in the bedroom, the children asleep, she unknitted her lips and words poured from her, black as pitch.

7

You Know Bert I Sometimes Marvel Women Can Go Sour Like That

Rex wondered if there were not something terribly wrong with Irene. He'd heard of women who went mental when they had babies. There was that woman from Ardlethan who took her toddlers aged three and five out the back of her house to a dam and drowned them. Held 'em under. It was on the radio for weeks. The strange part was she expressed no remorse; they hanged her in the Bathurst Gaol. Good riddance, said everyone.

Rex knew so little about the female sex. He searched his mind. His dominant memory of his mother was her corsets, which she wore even on the hottest days. And the sloshing chamber pot that she emptied every morning, always taking care to hide the offending liquid with a piece of newspaper before beginning the journey from the bedroom to the yard.

8

Home Is the First and Final Poem

It was not in Rex to exhibit temper, but sometimes, goaded by Irene's taunts, he saw red. At the top of his voice, he informed her that he was not asking much. All he wanted was to harvest his crops, care for his animals, share it all with a good woman.

Mostly, though, he just stood there, arms dangling. "Have a heart, Irene," he would say. "Have a heart."

9

I Am Not a Slut, Though I Thank the Gods I Am Foul

The first time Irene was unfaithful, it was by proxy. She wrote a letter to the American soldier—her Yank from the war—informing him of the birth of her boy and declaring that she wished it was his. She wished it so much that she had given the baby his name. And when she was finished, she left the letter in an unsealed envelope on top of the desk in the sitting room where Rex could not help but find it.

He read the letter in an agony of disbelief, yet without surprise; so altered was his world, he could not remember ever being innocent of its contents. That day, he went about his work without knowing what he was doing, blood roaring in his head.

He thought about leaving her. He knew men who had done that, left their wives and gone north, to Queensland or the Northern Territory, where they became shearers, roustabouts, boundary riders, kangaroo shooters—cranky characters spouting bush philosophy, eloquent on the subject of the female sex and their treacherous ways. Some tried their luck again and started new families, but they were never to be trusted: they knew how to padlock their consciences and make for the horizon.

He decided to stay.

10

In Sicily, the Black, Black Snakes Are Innocent, the Gold Are Venomous

With ample water and sun, not to mention a steady supply of cow manure, Irene's irises thrived. They were mostly the tall bearded variety, with generous, full-lipped flowers: white with yellow veining; delicate lilac; deepest purple.

Irene lined the children up and explained the botany of irises to them. The children, tiny and obedient, listened hard. The lesson over, she gave them another one on life.

"Unlike people, flowers never disappoint," she said, fixing on something in the middle distance.

An adult hearing this might have snorted with laughter, but the children only grew more solemn, pursing their lips and squinting up at her. Her meaning was beyond them. Flowers? Disappointment? All they knew was that she was their sun. If only she would stop radiating unhappiness!

At such moments, they tugged at her skirts, patted her. Sometimes, in the confusion of emotions that her shifting moods induced in them, they whimpered.

11

Wonderful! Wonderful!

Irene's next infidelity was at a Saturday night dance at the Catholic Club in Yoogali that she and Rex attended with a party of friends: Gladys and Reggie, Winifred and Charlie, Dulcie and George, Avis and Hans. With the exception of Avis, who worked at the Commonwealth Bank, and Hans, who was a superphosphate salesman, they were all from farms. They sat around a table, awkwardly at first, in couples, drinking ponies of beer and smoking Craven As, until the first dance, which gave them the opportunity to rearrange the table into a more comfortable configuration, men with men, women with women, teasing remarks batted between the two groups like shuttlecocks.

At intervals around the hall, doors opened onto purple darkness, allowing the weedy, mud-spiked smell of irrigation water to waft in and mingle with the cigarette smoke. Hans asked Irene to dance, and Rex followed suit with Avis. The band was playing a medley of Johnny Mathis tunes, and Hans amused Irene by singing the lyrics into her ear:

> *It's not for me to say you love me*
> *It's not for me to say you'll always care*

She smiled, moved closer. He gave her a narrow look, assessing her.

> *Perhaps the glow of love will grow*
> *With every passing day*
> *Or we may never meet again*
> *But then, it's not for me to say.*

They came to a door, and Hans dexterously swung her through it. Rex and Avis were up front near the band, a crush of dancers obscuring their view, but so masterful were Hans's movements, they might not have noticed even if they had been watching.

"Cha cha cha," said Hans, when they were on the other side of the door. They giggled, and Irene stumbled. He righted her, holding her by the elbow. Down the rows of cars they went until they reached the outer edge. In a nearby ditch, cicadas drummed.

Irene began to chatter—the cicadas, the plentiful stars—but Hans silenced her by pushing her against a car. He rucked up her skirt, pulled down her underpants. It was over in moments, but she reveled in the act, which she found to be deliciously obliterating, and also the adventure of it—the surreptitiousness, the deceit—which made her heart race. Years later she would remember the feel of the cold metal against her bare backside.

12

For the Term of Her Natural Life

Look at that lovely red canna." They were driving by the War Memorial Park. Irene braked, jumped out, the children trailing. She bent to uproot some canna bulb.

"No, Mum, don't! You'll be arrested!" Girlie hopped from one foot to the other.

"Oh, shut up," said Irene. A portion of bulb came suddenly free. She staggered, regained her balance.

13

Aitape

In the desk in the living room, behind family documents and income-tax papers, was a pair of yellow ivory chopsticks in a narrow wooden box with a sliding top. It was easily the most exotic object in the house, with far more allure than the trio of ebony elephants on the mantelpiece, bought by Rex in a bazaar in Aden, or the piano stool with legs that ended in claws grasping cloudy glass balls.

"Found 'em on a dead Jap up in New Guinea."

"Did you kill him?" Girlie and Boy were beside themselves. Dark jungles loomed, populated by Papua-New Guineans with frizzed hair and bones through their noses.

"No, I didn't kill him. Go on. Go away. Go and play."

"Did you kill *any* Japs?"

"Go and play."

Rex refused to talk about the war with anyone, not just the children. He marched on Anzac Day, down the main street of Progress, his medals pinned to his chest, but always remained silent when other farmers at the Returned Services League Club reminisced about the war. If Irene played "A Wing and a Prayer" on the piano on those evenings when they invited couples over for cards, he slipped from the room. If pressed, he said, "What would I want to talk about that for?"

14

The Biggest Fool

Girlie and Boy were at school and Rex and Irene were in the kitchen when an army mate of Rex's turned up unannounced. They heard his footsteps on the verandah.

"I was in the district. Asked around. Hope you don't mind."

"Oh no, not at all. Good to see you. Fancy that. Look who's here, Irene."

Irene's eyes went flat. For once, Rex didn't give a damn. Instead of asking Irene to make more tea, he went to the pantry and fetched the wicker-covered demijohn that held the sherry they served up as refreshment on card nights.

"Have some plonk," said Rex to his old friend. Glasses were filled, clinked together. The sherry was heavy and sweet, with a pronounced meniscus.

At first they talked only about recent events, what they had done with themselves as civvies and the fates of the men they knew. Eventually, they fell to swapping yarns about the war. Rex didn't resist; he was squiffy from the sherry.

The two men talked a blue streak, interrupting and finishing each other's sentences, as women do. Every now and again, one of them pushed back his chair and went out to the garden to relieve himself on Irene's crepe myrtle. By the middle of the afternoon, the kitchen table was sticky with plonk. "We're drunk as skunks," they chorused, by this time finding their every utterance a source of amusement.

Irene hovered at the kitchen sink, listening to the men's conversation and staring at her garden. For Lent, she had decided to drink her tea cold, with no milk and sugar, a version of sackcloth that she had come to like. As the day progressed, she drank a quantity of this bitter brew, pouring it from a teapot that stood on the sill above the sink. She grew increasingly jittery, in counterpoint to the men's relaxed inebriety.

Girlie and Boy came home from school. Something was wrong. Girlie sensed it before she was at the gate. In the kitchen, her father and a strange man. Her father's face was flushed, and he stank of sherry and scratched his crotch as if nobody else were there. She had never seen him like this. He was telling the story of his only brush with the law.

"We were at a pub in Crows Nest. It's raining, and we've had a few. I go to hail a taxi. There's one coming. I can see the light on top. It doesn't stop. So I whistle and yell, I jump up and down like a madman. That works all right. Blow me down if it isn't a police car."

Rex stopped, conscious of the children standing in the doorway. He lurched out of his chair.

"Here's my bonny lass. Come and dance with me, lassie."

Girlie ducked.

Boy hugged the wall, trying to make himself invisible so he could listen to the men's stories, but it was too late; his father's friend was taking his leave. They were both unsteady, so the army mate flung an arm around Rex, and he likewise, and they proceeded awkwardly through the door and onto the verandah, trailed by Irene, Girlie, and Boy.

They forsook the steps and made for the edge, where they fell off and landed in a heap on the lawn. They picked themselves up, giggling like girls. Proximity sparked their next idea: they must dance a tango. Heads together, arms leading at a stiff right angle, they pranced down the lawn. And fell in another heap.

Irene, Girlie, and Boy were lined up on the verandah watching this spectacle. Irene, hopped up on caffeine, was genuinely amused; she had been mollified by some complicitous glances that had passed between her and the army mate. She laughed, throwing back her head, as if this were the funniest thing she had ever seen. Girlie turned red and kicked herself in the ankle; she found what was happening unbearable. Boy's eyes tracked from his mother to his father and back again and then took his mother's lead and brayed like a little donkey.

15

Sex Is the Big Preoccupation of My Life, and Why Not?

Rex borrowed a bull to service his cows. The bull came crated on the back of a truck, a self-satisfied brute with stupid eyes. Girlie loitered near the water tank, hoping nobody would notice her. She didn't know why she shouldn't advertise her presence, except that every time the subject of the bull came up, voices were lowered. Boy was there, too, running around, getting underfoot.

Neighbors had dropped by to help: Cecil, Ernie, Roy, in blue overalls and heavy work boots. They had a purposeful air; this was serious work. Men's work. A ramp was attached to the truck, and the bull came down it gingerly, urged along by the men; they yelled and poked at his flanks with sticks.

"Ya ya ya ya."

"Ho. Ho. Gittalong."

The ramp bowed under the bull's weight.

"Hurry it up."

The bull reached the bottom of the ramp and surveyed the scene, taking his time, betraying no agitation. He had the comportment of a dictator: magisterial, mean. The cows, unsettled by the noise, had removed themselves to a far corner of the paddock. At that moment, Girlie saw what she was not supposed to see: the bull's penis, unsheathed, livid, huge. Girlie stole away. Boy caught sight of the bull's penis at the exact same moment: His eyes bugged out of his head.

16

Kangaroo Among the Beauty

Irene made Girlie a skirt for "dressing up" from an old evening gown. The fabric was shot silk. Girlie, who was literal-minded to a degree unusual even in a child, searched for pellet holes. That obstacle overcome, she was captivated by the cloth, twisting it in the light, slanting it, to change the color. Green, blue, bronze. She imagined a ballroom filled with exquisitely courteous men and women: deferential nods, sweeping bows, soft voices, cocked heads, playful laughs.

Whenever a song she found suitable came on the radio—"Volare," "Mountain Greenery"—Girlie raced to pull on the skirt and waltz around the kitchen table. She whirled faster and faster, her face blotching, until she was in danger of losing her balance. By the song's end, Girlie was dancing not to the music but to a manic rhythm suggested by her own hot blood.

Irene was irked by many things her daughter did, but this, she said, took the cake.

17

Hillbilly Music

It was late, around midnight, and in the shadows on the ceiling of Boy's room, the Battle of Britain was being fought, Spitfires in dogfights with Messerschmitts, Flying Fortresses and Blenheim Bombers droning across the English Channel. They were model airplanes hanging from nylon fishing line. Fiddly bits of plastic glued to plastic, faithful in detail down to decals and the number of guns in the turrets.

The household was asleep, except for Boy, who was under the blankets, where it was warm and sharp-smelling, like a fox's lair. He was listening to his transistor radio, a Grundig, his pride and joy, which was tuned to a station playing country music. Hank Williams was singing, "Hey, Good-Looking." Boy liked the man's nasal voice, the economy of his message, his restraint. The radio was Boy's school. He learned about life from it, the best he could.

Boy was exactly the child that Irene wanted, sturdily masculine, with a winning manner. He was a great one for agreeing with you and then doing as he wanted.

They enjoyed each other, mother and son. They laughed a lot.

18

Sticks and Stones
and Wallaby Bones

Girlie was the opposite of Boy: eager, earnest, graceless. She threw herself into everything, whether she was good at it or not, whether she enjoyed it or not.

Nobody liked her. Children thought she was a know-it-all, adults recoiled from her neediness. She cornered anyone she could and read them her compositions, which were of epic proportions and always featured a girl like herself—a *fearless* girl—having improbable adventures: captaining a submarine in the Arctic Circle or a junk in the China Seas. Girlie numbered her books and kept everyone up to date on the current figure.

Rex was no help to Girlie. He wanted to tell her not to try so hard but never found the opportunity. Rex was permanently distracted. He was like a character in a Wild West movie who is made to dance by means of bullets fired around his feet.

19

Varanus Giganteus

Rex believed a country woman should be able to do everything her husband could and more. In keeping with this policy, he announced over porridge that Girlie was to help him kill a rooster. This meant chopping off the head, plunging the body into scalding water so that the feathers could be plucked easily, eviscerating it. The mess afterward was terrible, with feathers and globs of gut everywhere. Once, a headless bird had flapped loose from Rex's hands and run in useless, frantic circles; even Boy was more appalled than entertained.

Water was put on the stove, and the stump used as a chopping block placed on the lawn. Girlie stood on the verandah and watched the preparations. She couldn't speak or move; she was paralyzed with revulsion. The rooster lay in the shade of an ornamental grapevine, its legs bound, struggling feebly.

"Here, Girlie. Come and hold it. Like this." Rex laid the bird across the stump. "I'll do the honors with the axe."

Suddenly Girlie was running down the path, slamming the gate, hightailing it across the paddocks. She inched under barbwire fences, crashed through stubble, eventually hiding in a clump of box trees, where she stayed all day, concealing herself whenever the utility truck came near, the sheep dogs in the back, Rex calling her name. Eventually, around dusk, under cover of the lengthening shadows, she crept home and lay on her bed, feigning sleep.

Rex hauled her off the bed. He rarely cuffed his children, but he had been out of his mind with worry. He yelled at her until she howled; he shook her so hard her head wobbled on her shoulders.

Rex decided that what would cure Girlie of her rebelliousness was a dose of Epsom salts. He was a great believer in Epsom salts, to cleanse the bowel but also to spruce up the spirit. With a large enough dose, a morose person could be made sunny overnight. He mixed a tablespoon of the stuff in warm water, and Girlie scrunched up her face to swallow it.

"You're as ugly as a goanna when you do that," said Rex, to check tears.

The Epsom salts had the desired effect: Girlie's

feces turned to water and gushed from her. Mortified, she positioned a chair outside the toilet and stubbornly sat there until her stomach stopped cramping, ignoring her family, who ribbed her: "Got the trots, have you, Girlie?"

Later, Girlie, with the odor of excrement still in her nose, examined her face in a mirror and had no trouble at all making out the boiled, folded features of a goanna.

20

Sock It to Me

Rex had a soft spot for pigs. He appreciated their intelligence and thoroughness. He had in mind to buy a dozen or so. Fatten 'em up, sell 'em. Easy money. He needed, however, to confine them; otherwise they would turn the farm into a dust bowl. To do this, he erected an electric fence, which had only three strands of wire. The outer two were harmless, but the middle one delivered a kick.

Despite graphic descriptions of what would happen if he touched the middle wire—char like a chop!—Boy could not stay away from the fence. At every opportunity, he set out for it, always by an indirect route but ending up in its vicinity. Once there, he played a form of Russian roulette by touching first the top wire and then the bottom, the top, the bottom. Eventually, it happened: In a moment of inattention, he touched the middle wire. When he opened his eyes, he was lying on his back, looking at white sky.

The pigs never materialized. Rex had kept his pig-farming plans from Irene, and when she found out, she put her foot down.

21

Secret to the Earth, Sowed by No One

Another favorite food of Irene's was mushrooms, which she sautéed slowly in flour and butter until they swam in a thick grey gravy. The mushrooms could be found in the winter months in a low-lying pocket of unploughed land. The trees that grew there had black bark and threw a deep shade, and the grass under them was always a delicate mint-green. The mushrooms were white on top, velvety brown underneath, and sometimes as large as saucers. Finding one never failed to elicit surprise; several paces away the soil turned unwilling and had to be coaxed to germinate anything other than burrs and thistles.

As soon as the children were old enough for such expeditions, Irene buttoned their cardigans, gave them a basket, and sent them across the paddocks. Girlie strode purposefully, gumboots slapping against her legs, determined to acquit herself, while Boy trailed behind, distracted by everything. He swung on gates, took imaginary aim at birds, kicked ant nests to smithereens, pelted paddymelons at fence posts.

One cloudy day in May, proceeding in this fashion, the children arrived at the edge of the depression. The trees murmured, faint and low. Before they could find any mushrooms, they came across the remains of a dead sheep. The head and hooves were gone, only the fleece lay there, spread out invitingly, like a rug before a fireplace. Sun had bleached the wool, rain washed it clean; it dazzled as if in an advertisement.

"Let's take it home and give it to Mum," said Girlie.

Boy did not say anything. He took a stick and poked experimentally at the fleece, as if expecting the sheep to reconstruct itself and run off. He lifted an edge, revealing something that resembled the padding placed under carpet to give it spring. The padding moved, swarmed. Maggots.

22

The Bravest Thing
God Ever Made!

irlie wrote a composition on Simpson and his donkey, and it won first prize in a Returned Services League competition. She painted a vivid picture of the sea at Gallipoli streaked with the blood of Australian soldiers, the cliffs strewn with their broken bodies. Behind tangles of barbed wire, she placed the enemy: black-eyed Turks. And in the middle of the mayhem, the doughty Simpson carrying the wounded on his donkey, shells bursting around them. She used words like "intrepid," "tenacious," and "selfless," and imagined herself to have some of these virtues.

A ceremony was held at school where she was presented with an oversized book of photographs of the Royal Family: crowns, scepters, sashes, ermine-trimmed robes, gold-encrusted coaches, ladies-in-waiting, but also "casual" shots of Charles in a kilt playing with the corgis and Anne in a sprigged frock bending to smell a rose.

Girlie was invited to read her prize-winning composition on the radio as part of the Anzac Day observances. Irene accompanied her. Freddie Garlick, who ran the radio station, tried to put Girlie at her ease. He adjusted the microphone, pushed the chair close. She read with a reedy voice, lisping slightly, the paper shaking in her hands.

When the program was over, Freddie accompanied them to the front door. "Keep up the good work," he said to Girlie. His tone of voice was such that Girlie thought it quite possible he didn't mean either that it was good work or that she should keep doing it. Then he said, "Your socks are falling down." Girlie hurriedly bent to attend to them, pitching forward in the process. Freddie said to Irene, "I like your style. You wear your dresses as if they were Paris couture." And it was true that Irene had a proud walk.

23

Send My Roots Rain

At night, Rex tossing beside her, skewing the bedclothes, Irene thought of fleeing. It should be easy, a "cinch," as Americans might say: a suitcase of clothes, a train to Sydney. She pictured herself boarding the train, stowing her suitcase in the rack, placing her feet on a tin footwarmer, closing the window against cinders. Irene loved to travel. To be going somewhere. Anywhere. Recklessness stirred in her.

As the train neared Sydney, though, her imagination failed. Instead of the platform at Central Station, solid under weary legs, there was a chasm. Instead of a new life, instead of possibilities— nothing. In her frustration, another image filled her mind: a penned heifer. Irene's heifer was in the pink of health, with gleaming flanks, strong teeth, pointy hooves, but its muzzle was flecked with foam, and its eyes swiveled to the side, to the back of its head. Irene wept for herself.

She cast around for a solution closer to home. A job, perhaps. In Progress, women worked in the banks, postoffice, library, hospital, and schools, although they gave it up once they had children. Irene particularly envied the women scientists posted to the agricultural research laboratories near Progress, but they were unmarried and had university degrees; another species, as far as she was concerned. No one would employ her.

Still, the idea of working stayed with her, so when Freddie Garlick offered her a dogsbody position—typing, filing, answering the phone—she jumped at the chance. Rex approved; anything to make her happy. He bought her a Volkswagen—white, with baby-blue upholstery—and the eagerness with which she put on her lipstick and climbed into the little car to go to work every morning was pitiful. The neighbors thought it was one more example of Irene getting above herself.

24

And You Alone Can Hear
the Invisible Starfall

Frederick Garlick was an ugly man—
small, swarthy, jug-eared—with a reso-
nant voice and boundless energy. A mongrel, he
said, to forestall questions about his looks. A bit of
everything: Scottish, Portuguese, Polish, even some
gypsy blood. He was a type occasionally found in rural towns: well-educated, lacking not in ideas but direction. Or, rather, he had gone in too many
directions, to find himself the manager of a country radio station. All the same, he was making the
best of it.

After Irene had been at the radio station several
days, Freddie invited her into the second of the station's two studios, a tiny cork-lined windowless
room. Although Freddie's sexuality was as indeter-
minate as his parentage—a born bachelor was the

general consensus—Irene hoped for seduction. Instead, he asked her to sit.

"Listen," he said.

With infinite care, he lowered the arm of the turntable onto a record, and the opening bars of Beethoven's "Emperor" Concerto crashed from the speakers. He handed her the sleeve of the record, which was decorated with a large gold crown on a red background, and she sat holding it and listening.

The pianist was Arthur Rubinstein, with the orchestra conducted by Josef Krips. By the end of the second movement, she was in tears. Here was something that expressed exactly her own feelings of yearning and dread. Here was something to which she could tie her turbulence.

Freddie hated Bach, Handel, and Mozart, loved Beethoven, Rachmaninoff, Shostakovitch, Rimsky-Korsakov, and Liszt, and these became Irene's favorite composers; his tastes suited her perfectly. He didn't restrict his instruction to music; he played her a recording of *Under Milk Wood,* and again doors opened for Irene. She exulted in the tumble of Dylan Thomas's words, relished his bawdy puns. He gave her volumes of poetry by Constantine Cavafy and George Seferis, and she dreamed of visiting Greece.

Culture did not sweeten Irene, or make her wise. Instead, the more she was exposed to it, the more crabbed her spirit became. She had always felt superior; now she had reason. Fate had been cruel to marry her to a farmer. Such a dull, mean, ordinary existence! She chewed on the injustice of it like a dog with a piece of hide.

25

The Pleasant Place of All Festivity

The event that confirmed Boy once and for all in the view that it was best not to show enthusiasm was a carnival Freddie organized. He had the bright idea that Progress, instead of parading floats down the main street like every other town, should have a water carnival. There was a stretch of cement-lined canal between the showground and municipal offices that was perfect for such an occasion. Freddie had political ambitions.

When told of this, Boy hatched a plan to make a gondola. He labored on the project for months, mounting a gondola-shaped plywood frame on an old beat-up rowboat that his father used on duck-shooting expeditions; the contraption then received a coat of silver paint. The finishing touch: a canopy decorated with purple crepe-paper flowers.

Every boat, no matter how modest, needs a name. Freddie suggested "Bella." Beautiful, like your mother, he explained. And that was what Boy painted on its side.

When the big day arrived, Rex loaded Boy's creation onto the tray of his Bedford truck and drove the whole family into Progress. After breaking a bottle of pilsner on its prow, they all helped push the gondola into the water, then stood back and held their breaths. It floated!

Freddie, in a red waistcoat and tasseled cap, stood in the back of the gondola, poling it along. Irene sat under the canopy and assumed a royal pose. Don't we look proper idiots, they had said, as they set off, giggling like maniacs and setting the boat wobbling. They told each other they were doing it for Boy, who had put so much effort into building the thing.

Boy had positioned himself in front of the crowd on the canal bank, the better to enjoy his triumph. As the gondola drew near, he began to wave. Then he saw himself as if from a distance: a boy waving like a *dickhead* at his mother in a *pretend* gondola. He pushed his way through the crowd and sat in the cab of the Bedford until it was time to go home.

26

Alive As Fire, and Evilly Aware

A small boy was walking along a bush track, hands stuck in his pockets, lips puckered in a whistle. Sunlight streamed through the leaves, dappling his path. His presence disturbed a flock of corellas, and they burst into the air, wheeling and whirring. The boy watched appreciatively, canting his head, shading his eyes, and then continued on his way, until he came to a log. He stepped over it, taking his hands out of his pockets, angling his body, for it was a large log. The snake struck with impersonal dispatch.

Exclamations of horror rose from the class. The boys started in their seats, the girls covered their eyes or wrung their handkerchiefs. The teacher, who was standing by the projector, hushed them, and they settled down to watch the rest of the film. The boy's whistling, the sounds of the bush, had been replaced by the voice of a narrator—male, grave, pedantic, the voice that ran the world. "Stuart was careless," the voice intoned. "He risked certain death."

Fortunately for Stuart, he had in his pocket what he needed to save himself: a razor blade. He also had presence of mind, which was the quality one needed above all others to survive the perils of the Australian bush, or so the narrator instructed the class. Using what remained of his strength—with every beat of his heart, the poison was coursing through his bloodstream, a fact borne home by the soundtrack, which thumped intimately—the boy tore a strip off his shirt and tied it around his thigh. He scrabbled in the dry leaves and found a stick, inserted it in the bandage on his leg and twisted until the cloth tightened into a tourniquet. Grimacing at the pain, he made a cut where the wound was and bent to suck out the poison.

The class gagged. Like all country children, they had learned from an early age to be watchful. There were no leopards, tigers, or bears in their surroundings, noble animals that rushed and growled and gave their victims a sporting chance, only stealthy, circumspect creatures like spiders, scorpions, and snakes.

The film was over, the blinds raised. The teacher read to her class from a natural-science textbook: "Australia has a larger proportion of venomous snakes than any other continent in the world, over seventy varieties. The species that kill include the death adder, the brown snake, the black snake, and the tiger snake. When milked, a single tiger snake produces enough poison to kill 118 sheep.''

The phrase "certain death" lodged in Girlie's brain, as did the statistic of 118 sheep. She lay in bed at night and imagined snakes, silent and purposeful, slithering up drainpipes, sliding through knotholes, into the house.

27

Tighter Breathing

Irene was keen on the natural sciences. She gave the children a Jacques Cousteau book featuring a photograph of a scuba-diver banging a shark on the snout with his camera, if you could believe that. She bought them another book on Australian fauna: lyrebirds, bandicoots, emus, platypuses, Tasmanian devils, and, of course, snakes.

Girlie had only to open the book on Australian fauna and her heart began to skip. As she approached the section on snakes, she turned the pages slower and slower, finally barely able to touch them. She forced herself to look. There they were, singly or in nests, coiled or grappling, some in camouflage colors, others banded like football players. Fanged, flickering, unblinking. She convinced herself that the glossy pages felt as the scales of a snake might.

28

Zero at the Bone

Rex was adept at decapitating snakes with his shovel. The body would lie in the milkweed and thistle at the side of a road or draped on the dirt shoulder of an irrigation channel, singing with insect life, guts slickly iridescent, scales dimming, until only flimsy skin remained, to be snagged by the wind on fencing or grass stalks, where it flapped for a time, bleaching to tissue, and disintegrated.

29

I Wish You Bluebirds

In 1959, Jack Davy, popular radio quiz master and host of the "Give It a Go" and "Ask Me Another" shows, died of a heart attack. That same year, Hildegarde Hochschwender arrived in Progress on a Harley Davidson motorbike, clear rubber-framed goggles covering her eyes and a windcheater zipped up to her chin. Attached to the motorbike was a sidecar carrying Audrey Jones, Hildegarde's friend of many years, also in goggles and windcheater.

Hildegarde was solidly built, with brown eyes and straight blunt-cut hair. Her voice, raspy and heavily accented, was disarmingly similar to Marlene Dietrich's. Audrey was Hildegarde's opposite: sharp features, freckles as large as threepenny bits on her face and arms, and an expression that was permanently suspicious. It was as if an otter and a crow had struck up a partnership. Hildegarde and Audrey sometimes walked with a small swagger, but usually only after dismounting from the motorbike.

Strangely enough, the couple did not attract comment. Not immediately. At that time the "hot" topic in Progress was the jeweler's son, apprehended for repeatedly trying to burn down St. Clement's. The fires had been set against the wall of the nave, an orderly arrangement of kindling and crunched-up pages from a hymnal; it was the neatness that made the police suspect the jeweler's son, who was the scout leader.

Rumors were also flying about a Russian family who lived on the edge of town. Black magic and strange sexual practices were hinted at, although the evidence was flimsy: the father had a goatee beard and read books printed in the Cyrillic alphabet, and there was a nubile daughter. The good people of Progress were careless with their slander.

The truth was that Hildegarde and Audrey were outside their ken. When the couple described themselves as old friends seeing the world, the response was, How adventurous! Privately, the two women were thought to be plain janes. Couldn't they do something to make themselves more attractive to men? A little lipstick—"lippie"—or a chiffon scarf knotted at the neck was prescribed.

Hildegarde and Audrey were tired of traveling and Progress seemed a likely place; they rented a flat above a shop, and Hildegarde found a job at the town newspaper, Audrey at the hospital. The newspaper office was next door to the radio station, so it wasn't long before Hildegarde and Irene met.

Irene was immediately attracted to Hildegarde, to her foreignness. Irene had no women friends. Even Billie had been dropped after the wedding, her letters unanswered. "You have to prune friendships," Irene told Girlie. Irene, notoriously savage with a pair of secateurs, pruned her tree of friendship within an inch of its life.

30

I Love My Love
with a Dress and a Hat

Lovers under the lap," said Freddie to Irene, who had brought him a cup of tea. He was on air, waiting for a song—"Purple People Eater," as it happened—to finish. They were discussing Hildegarde and Audrey.

"Lovers under the what?" asked Irene, startled.

"Diesels."

Irene stared at him hard.

"Lezzos."

"Oh."

"Need a diagram?"

"No."

"Johnny Mathis is a homo," said Freddie, one thing reminding him of another. What Freddie did when he went to Sydney was anybody's guess.

"I knew that," said Irene, who hadn't, and withdrew into thought.

31

Titan

Rex was happy that Irene had a friend. Hildegarde came around mostly on Saturday afternoons—Audrey was somehow always on duty at the hospital—and Hildegarde and Irene would sit leaning against the verandah posts listening to records: Beethoven, Liszt, Sibelius. In throaty tones, Hildegarde described the concert houses of Europe and conifer forests where the sun never shone; Irene was transfixed.

When it was Irene's birthday, Rex asked Hildegarde for advice as to what to give her, and she suggested Mahler's First Symphony, conducted by Bruno Walter. Rex ordered it from Rangott's Records on the main street of Progress, where Irene had purchased her record player, a portable model, grey with pink trim. When Irene took off the wrapping and saw the handsome boxed set, her smile was forgiving. For a time, Rex felt less useless.

Irene gathered Girlie and Boy around the record player and made them listen. In certain sections, if you concentrated, you could hear the conductor stamp his foot and grunt. Irene could barely contain her excitement as she waited for these moments. She did not view the extraneous noises as flaws. Instead, she was reassured by them. The music had not been handed down from Olympus; humans like herself had created it.

32

Fantasia

Girlie was not so sure about Bruno Walter's grunts. She'd had a disillusioning experience when the Arts Council ballet company came to town and performed for her school in the church hall. The taped music was tinny and piping, and dust rose with every pirouette, but to Girlie's eyes, the ballerinas were gossamer creatures. One in particular she thought ineffably beautiful, with doe eyes and a long neck.

After the performance, the audience was invited "backstage" to meet the "corps de ballet." Girlie went as if into the company of goddesses. The ballerina she had admired was taking off her pancake make-up with Pond's cold cream. Wads of cotton wool smeared with brown muck lay on a trestle table that normally held church suppers. To Girlie's distress, the ballerina had freckles and a prominent fleshy nose. Worse, she smelled strongly of sweat, like a horse after a workout. Girlie bowed her head. "Don't be shy," said the ballerina. Girlie blushed; she was feeling disgust.

33

She and I

Mysteriously, Hildegarde had no interest in Boy. She would pinch his cheek and ask about his model airplanes, and then turn to Girlie and ask if she wanted to go for a ride—"a burn"—on the bike. And Girlie would climb onto the pillion seat, carefully avoiding the exhaust pipe, and off they would go, Girlie's arms around the reassuring thickness of Hildegarde's waist, fences, houses, trees, telephone poles joining in a blur, until they reached bitumen, where Hildegarde cranked up the speed and Girlie's eyes began to water. Then she would turn her head to the side and place her cheek against Hildegarde's back.

34

Hist! Hark!

The nearest river to Progress was the Murrumbidgee, some seventy-five miles away. In winter, it was sulky, brown, and wide. In summer, the mud settled, and it became the same shade of green—soft, silvery—as the leaves of the tall, angular gums that jostled for room on its banks, dipping branches over the water like men doffing hats.

Irene and Hildegarde had been told of an isolated part of the river where there was a spit of sand and excellent swimming. Ready for adventure, they loaded a couple of old kapok mattresses into the car, along with mosquito nets, cooking utensils, and a canvas water bag, and set off with the children, planning to camp out for two nights. Rex stayed behind to play cricket.

They found the spot after a few wrong turnings.

The river was low and lazy, its steep chalky banks exposed. Water swirled silently around the trunks of upended trees, victims of attrition and winter floods. The air smelled of wet clay and eucalyptus leaves; flies formed clouds.

They swam and then prepared for the night, hanging the mosquito nets from the branches of trees at the sand's edge, placing the mattresses under them. Kindling was collected, a fire lit in a scooped-out hole on the beach. They ate sausages and drank billy tea, and then the children were sent to bed, where they lay wide-awake, watching Irene and Hildegarde, who sat on a log and talked as the fire burned to coals.

Irene and Hildegarde's voices echoed in the stillness. Girlie and Boy strained to make sense of their conversation; they could tell who was speaking but not what was said. After a bit—the children sat up, sensing that something unusual was about to happen—Irene and Hildegarde left the fire and went down to water's edge, where they undressed. Their naked bodies shone against the dark river, luminous and indefinite as ghosts.

Splashing, laughter. One of them—their mother, from the pitch of the voice—did a war dance in the shallow water, whooping, lifting her legs up, running in circles. Her cries bounced off the river, into the tops of the trees, startling roosting birds. Then the two women went out deeper, gliding into blackness, making no sound at all; the only thing the children could see were the trees on the opposite bank, hulked against a pearly night sky.

Boy filed the event under "interesting," to be thought about at a later date, and went to sleep. Girlie tossed and turned, ears alert. Leaves rustled. A bird flapped. She dozed, to wake with a start. Something was pushing against the mosquito net. Girlie screamed, and Irene and Hildegarde, pulling on clothes, came running.

It was a cow, one of a herd drifting to the river to drink.

35

Love's Always Been My Game

ASaturday afternoon, Hildegarde was visiting. Boy came through the gate from the home paddock, a magpie chick in his cupped hands. He had found it in the grass underneath an ancient cypress pine, its beak wide open, but no noise issuing. He showed the creature to his father, who was on his way to the garage to soak a cricket bat in linseed oil, and asked him if the chick could be returned to its nest.

"Waste of time," said Rex.

"I will climb," said Hildegarde.

Irene, Hildegarde, and Boy trooped to the paddock. This was fun, such good fun! Hildegarde zipped her windcheater part way up, nestled the bird next to her chest. She shinnied up the trunk, hoisted herself into the lower branches.

"Careful, Hildegarde."

"In Germany, as children, we played in trees like this."

Unlike the trees of her youth, the bark of the Australian cypress pine was rough and furrowed. It bit into her hands. The tree was also higher than she had estimated. Hildegarde would have liked to have beat a retreat, but her honor was at stake.

The bird was eventually installed in its nest. Back on the ground, a fuss was made over Hildegarde's scratches.

Wiping his hands on a rag, Rex emerged from the garage, next to which was an almond tree flounced with blossoms. He happened to look up just as the women leaned their heads together. Hildegarde said something, Irene laughed in reply. From the kitchen window, that damn music.

Rex strode over and stood in front of Hildegarde, who knew in a flash what was coming.

"Get out of here," he yelled, veins bulging, spit flying. "I don't want to see you in my house again."

The next day, Boy found the magpie chick again lying in the grass at the bottom of the old cypress pine, but this time it was dead, its papery corpse covered with ants. Boy was obscurely pleased. He picked the bird up by a claw, hurled it into the air.

36

Vengeance Is Mine

Rex ranted from time to time about how Girlie was ruining her eyes from reading. "Go outside, lassie. Enjoy life while you're young," he'd exhort.

Girlie read books like a caterpillar eating its way through the leaves on a tree. For some time she had been hungrily eyeing her mother's bookshelf, but Irene had declared it out of bounds. The attraction grew stronger, and one morning before school Girlie stole *Anna Karenina* off the shelf. It was either that or *Peyton Place*. Her daring turned her legs to jelly. She hid the book—a Penguin Classic, with an orange spine—in her case. On the school bus she made a great show of reading it while the others leafed through comic books and *True Confession* magazines or studied for tests.

She continued reading it through the day, concealing it in her lap during classes. It made little sense to her, the ant-like words, the explosive Russian names, the to-ings and fro-ings, the convoluted declarations of love. The train journeys, however, were familiar from the long trips Irene, Boy, and herself had made to Sydney to visit relatives. The thrill of journeying—cold railway platforms, sooty smoke, shuntings and clangings—this she could grasp.

Girlie was called on to answer a question in a mathematics class, and she shoved the book into the ink-stained, paper-littered interior of the desk. She remembered it as she sat down for the next class. When she went to retrieve the book, it was gone. Every day for months she expected Irene to remark on the book's absence; her guilt became a brace that bit into her whenever she relaxed. Irene never said a word.

37

They Say All Things Are for the Best

As he made his rounds, on land that he would never own, Rex droned the chorus of a song he had learned in the army:

Jim crack corn, I don't care.
Jim crack corn, I don't care.
Jim crack corn, I don't care.
Ol' master's gone away.

That was the extent of his repertoire. His dogs, soft-eyed and wet-nosed, attentive to his every gesture, were always by his side. If he went anywhere in his utility, they piled into the back, panting and slobbering. When the vehicle was in motion, they faced into the wind, eyes half-closed, pink tongues flapping like flags. At night, he chained them to kennels in the tractor shed, where they waited patiently for his return in the morning. "Faithful as the night is long," said Rex of his dogs.

One of the dogs was called Flash, after Flash Gordon, and the other was Emma, after a television character played by Diana Rigg, whom Rex rather fancied. Television had recently come to the district, and Rex had taken to the medium, planting his armchair in front of the set, applying himself to it with the same seriousness with which he read the local newspaper.

The dogs' attentiveness did not extend to obedience. Keeping the sheep bunched in tight, manageable groups was beyond them. Nor did they run agilely across the backs of penned sheep, as one sometimes saw in newsreels proclaiming Australia's might as a wool-producing country. Because of this, a session in the sheepyards was a cacophony of yaps, yelps, yells: "Goddamn it, Flash, get over here!" "Jesus Christ, Emma!"

Then came the terrible day when the utility was at the garage being fitted with new tires, and Rex used the family sedan to check on some sheep at the far end of the farm. He took Emma with him, and her paws got muddy; on the return journey he put her in the boot so she wouldn't dirty the seats. When he reached the house, he was distracted by a minor crisis, and when he remembered Emma half an hour later—it was a hot day—she was dead.

38

In Accents Most Forlorn

In the winter of 1964, the mice came in never-ending grey waves. They were everywhere, in shoes and boots, the stove, the toaster, even the electric jug. Move something, pick it up—a bag of wheat, a bale of hay—and mice exploded into furious action, darting in a hundred different directions, like living shrapnel. The air was fusty with their smell.

The dogs grew dizzy chasing bolting mice and soon adopted poses of indifference. The cats—pet and feral—had only to open half an eye to see their next meal. Goannas gorged until they could barely haul their swaying bodies up trees. Snakes satiated themselves, becoming lethargic, slow as slugs.

At night, before going to bed, Rex stretched a tarpaulin on the ground and in the morning poked a hose under it. The hose was attached to the exhaust of the utility, whose engine he duly started. Thousands of mice expired each time. He shoveled them into a trench, added dirt as if layering a cake. Months after the plague ended, Rex could still see mice out of the corners of his eyes: blurred, teeming.

39

Dust Shalt Thou Eat

Clouds of dust boiling in from the west.

The trees in the near distance were obliterated first, then the sheds, the water tank, the windmill, the cypress pine, the fence to the yard. The sun was also obscured; the light became yellow, gloomy. The family watched at the kitchen window as sheets of corrugated iron and roly-polies whipped by.

Dust filtered into the house, clogging their nostrils; they champed on the stuff. Soon the house was veiled with dust; it lay an inch thick on horizontal surfaces, but it also clung to the walls, the ceiling, the sides of the refrigerator.

40

The Brief Lives of Insects

Avenging clouds again, this time of locusts. From a distance, the clouds emitted a steady thrumming sound; up close, in their midst, the noise broke into its component parts: clickings and scrapings as well as the whirring of a hundred million wings. Rex's barley crop was a victim, as was Irene's garden. The locusts smashed blindly into windows, daubing them with their viscous entrails, which dried to a gluelike hardness. Rex sprayed insecticide, and the bodies of those felled crunched underfoot.

41

Mercy Mercy Mercy

Stones on the roof. Someone was showering stones on the roof. Dimly awake, Rex thought it was his brother, playing a trick, and then he knew what it was: hail heavy enough to flatten the wheat crop. The children came without being summoned. The four of them stood in the living room in their pajamas staring up at the ceiling, as if that could provide answers. Rex drew back a curtain and shone a torch outside: the ground was white with hail. And still it came: pelting, pinging, skidding.

"Say goodbye to the wheat," said Rex.

"The insurance will pay," said Irene, the same words she had used about the locusts. The children nodded in agreement, their teenage faces fatuously solemn. Rex looked at his wife, baffled anew by her insensitivity. Of course the insurance will pay. That wasn't the point; his work was shredded.

42

Life-writing

Girlie hardly noticed the scourges visited upon the farm. She was captive to her mother's every mood, quivering to them like a tuning fork. At the smallest provocation, Irene cut her daughter off, and it drove Girlie half-mad. When communication resumed, Girlie could never quite get it right; out of uncertainty, she was apt to be fulsome and giddy.

Boy was no more observant of his natural environment than his sister. His energies went into practicing neutrality; he kept his head low, cloaked himself in ordinariness. His interests were typical of a teenage boy: movies, music, sports, sex. If he had aspirations, apart from a desire not to be a farmer, no one knew.

Irene, however, was busy noticing everything. Freddie had given her an old Remington portable, and she had discovered that she had a way with words. Using as her model the American humorist Betty MacDonald, whose book *The Egg and I* was enjoying a vogue, she wrote vignettes about the farming life that were upbeat and rueful. First she read them on the radio, and then the local newspaper gave her a column.

Using understatement typical of farmers, Rex admitted to neighbors that he thought Irene's columns were "a bit rich"; he read them shaking his head.

43

Close Your Eyes

S chinus molle. Anacardiaceae family," said Irene. She was in the bath, soapy water lapping at her shoulders, legs bent so that her knees made islands, a flannel floating in the vicinity of her bosom for modesty's sake, and she was instructing her son, who was sitting on top of a cupboard that held towels, in the taxonomy of the pepper tree they could both see framed in the open bathroom door.

"It's not a native, you know, although it looks like it has been here forever, under our beastly sun. Its common name is the California pepper tree, but it doesn't come from California, either. Comes from Peru. We gave the Americas eucalypts, they gave us pepper trees." She inclined her head, admiring the tree's twisted trunk and clusters of tiny bright pink berries.

Boy, who had been enduring his mother's botanical lessons for years, said nothing. It was dim in the bathroom, cavelike, cool. Outside: the tired late-afternoon light of a summer's day.

The bathroom was the one room in the house that remained unchanged. The tin walls were rippled and painted an institutional green, the floor was cement. The tub, large and clawed, was also green. The ceiling was high, beyond the reach of a broom; daddy-long-legs wove dense webs in the corners.

The two of them had fallen into the habit of having chats while Irene took baths when Boy was five or six and had never given it up, even after Boy's voice broke and his body grew lanky. In these sessions, Irene sometimes interrogated Boy about school, books he was reading, friends, girls, but what they liked best to do was recite snatches of banter they had picked up from here and there and polished into routines. The Goon Show was a popular source of material, as was *Mad* magazine.

Irene moved, and water sloshed over the edge.

"More kindling, Boy."

The water was warmed by means of a chip heater, a primitive Australian invention consisting of a cylinder, where the fire was set, and a flue exiting through the roof. Boy took a jemmy and cautiously levered the lid off the heater, then dropped slivers of pine into the heater's belly. The fire flared almost immediately, and the contraption huffed like a train on a straight stretch.

Irene and Boy paid no attention to the lunatic noise issuing from the heater. When it was quiet again, Irene, in a nasal voice quite unlike her own, said, "Books are for the birds." She was pretending to be Paul McCartney's grandfather in *A Hard Day's Night*, which had been showing in Progress that last week. Paul's nasty old git of a grandfather tickled the two of them, and they had been twice.

Boy took the cue and became Ringo. "Books are good," he replied in his best Liverpudlian accent, dropping consonants and swallowing vowels as if born to it.

"Parading's better," said Paul's grandfather.

"Parading?" queried Ringo.

"Parading the streets, trailing your coat, bowling along. Living!" explained Paul's grandfather.

"I am living," said Ringo.

"You! Living! When was the last time you gave a girl a pink-edged daisy? When was the last time you embarrassed a sheila with a cool appraising stare," retorted Paul's grandfather.

Irene couldn't keep it up; she dissolved into laughter. She twisted her torso to throw the soap at Boy; the flannel slipped. While he wasn't so bold as to venture "a cool appraising stare," Boy stole a look at his mother. Irene knew he was looking; she rather enjoyed it. How else was he to learn? The soap missed Boy and banged against the tin wall.

Irene settled back in the water.

It was Ringo's turn. "Bit old for that sort of chat, aren't you?"

"Well at least I've got a backlog of memories. All you've got is a book," said Paul's grandfather.

But Irene'd had enough. When she spoke again, it was her normal voice. "Time you went, Boy. Before you go, put a few more chips in the heater. And find the soap, please."

Boy did her bidding. The fire blazed, the heater pulsed, hot water sputtered into the bath. Boy paused for a last bit of repartee. Over the noise of the heater, he shouted in Liverpudlian, "Clean old man!"

Boy was in the door, silhouetted; Irene couldn't make out the details of his face. "Don't press your luck," she shouted back, souring her features, Paul's grandfather to a T.

44

A Laughing Woman with
Two Bright Eyes

rene had a new friend. Her name was Gwyneth, and she was one of the women scientists at the agricultural research laboratories. Her area of expertise was rust in wheat. She had blonde hair and looked good in jodhpurs, which she wore as an affectation. "Where's the horse?" Rex couldn't resist asking, and Gwyneth laughed good-naturedly. It became a joke with them.

Gwyneth came to stay for a weekend, and in the middle of a restless moonlit night—the screeching of a cornered animal had set the dogs barking, waking them all—she slipped into Boy's bed and deftly undid the cord on his pajama pants. Not a word passed between them. Boy couldn't believe his luck. Afterward, he felt much the same as when he had touched the electric fence.

In one of their bathroom sessions, he told his mother what Gwyneth had done.

"How about that," said Irene.

45

The Imperative:
Snakes May Not Live

Boy saw him first. A brown snake. It was sunning itself on the path leading to the house. Had to be seven feet long. At least. A whopper. Boy picked up an axe and went after it, but the snake moved faster than seemed probable for its size. Boy smashed down on the concrete with the axe, missing the brute. And smashed down again. The snake seemed to be making for the gate but at the last moment veered into a bed of rose bushes, traversed a stretch of lawn, and disappeared among the tangle of roots at the base of the passion-fruit vine.

When it was over, Boy found he had gouged holes in the cement at regular intervals the full length of the path. When Rex saw the damage, he took off his hat and scratched the back of his head. "Stone the crows, Boy. Was that necessary?"

46

Passenger of My Passage

Girlie was walking along the narrow dirt path to the vegetable garden when her father called out, "Don't move, Girlie. Keep very still." A snake. Girlie's wits deserted her, took off for the hills. She was left hollow, staring, like a china doll.

Afterwards, Rex hunted the creature for over an hour, beating the grass, lifting back foliage, without success. He said that the snake—brown, slim, about five feet long—had been right beside her, moving very slowly, unconcerned about her presence, promenading!

Irene watched the goings-on with an air of bemusement. "*Poor* Girlie," she said, shaking her head, "such a scaredy-cat!" Irene had read somewhere that snakes were necessary to the balance of nature.

47

Telling Tales Is Telling Lies

Irene hated gossip, perhaps because she guessed she was the object of it. She could work herself into a lather of righteousness on the subject. Keep your own counsel, she warned the children, and told of dire consequences if they didn't.

Girlie repeated something Irene had said about a neighbor to her friends at school, and the remark made its way to the neighbor with the swiftness of an arrow. Irene was tending her sweet pea plants, tying loose tendrils to a trellis, when she saw the neighbor's car approaching, trailing a plume of dust of a size that indicated an accelerator pressed to the floor. The neighbor had a high old time acting the injured party; the role, for once, was reversed.

Girlie arrived home from school to find her mother in a cold fury. "You want to end up like them?" Irene asked. Her hand swept in an arc and took in Progress and environs. "You want to end up a *pygmy?*"

Girlie said she was sorry. Very sorry. Irene told her how to make reparations. Girlie should go to the top of a hill—she pointed in the direction of a protuberance to the west of Progress, hardly a hill, really, but it pleased the locals to think they had at least one distinctive geographical feature—and scatter a bag of feathers. When she had retrieved every last feather, Irene would accept her apology.

48

The Little Bearded Governess
Gazed Sadly at Her Basket of Tulips

Girlie had a new English teacher, an untidy, pimply young woman named Miss Boatwright, whom she couldn't stand. She became as impatient as her mother, shooting up her hand to point out the teacher's errors, creating disturbances, generally being delinquent. At recess, she made fun of the half-moons of sweat that stained the armpits of Miss Boatwright's frocks. Miss Boatwright was "common," Girlie said, and everyone agreed.

Miss Boatwright's efforts at salvaging her dignity only made Girlie more scornful. In her mind, she played out scenarios in which Miss Boatwright came to harm. She had done this sort of thing before, imagining her mother's death, the funeral, the reactions of people. She felt guilty, but Irene always said nobody could read thoughts; they were the only things that were truly your own.

49

One Candle Is Enough

Archdeacon Potts, in the pulpit, was asking for money to buy new Easter vestments. For a country priest, Archdeacon Potts had expensive tastes: lace, linen, chased metal.

Irene, sitting with Girlie and Boy, had closed her ears. She was thinking about Nick Pasquale, who had taken over from old Mr. Smith as the town's photographer. Freddie had introduced her to him. Nick was a loner: sloping, wolfish, withdrawn. Needless to say, Irene viewed him much as a safe-cracker might a safe.

Girlie wasn't listening to the priest, either. She was mentally ticking off the causes of the First World War in preparation for a history test the next day. For his part, Boy was already eating the roast dinner they would have when they returned home: lamb, potatoes, plenty of gravy.

"Hymn number ninety-three."

The congregation shuffled to their feet, shook their limbs free of pins and needles, coughed, rustled hymnals. Irene nudged Boy and smiled. It was a well-known hymn; they could all have "a good bellow," as Irene liked to put it:

> . . . *Christ, the royal Master,*
> *Leads against the foe;*
> *Forward into battle*
> *See, his banners go!*

One by one, they heard it: a snorting, snuffling sound. It was coming from the direction of the choir loft. A few people gamely kept singing; everyone else craned their necks. The snuffling became a keening, which was abruptly terminated by several loud thumps, followed by scuffling, then silence.

After the service, the congregation gathered on the church steps. The disturbance, it was soon learned, had been caused by Miss Boatwright, Girlie's English teacher. Miss Boatwright had been taken to the hospital. A fit, said a woman who had been in the choir loft. Heads bent toward each other, voices softened, turned sibilant.

Irene hurried the children past the gossiping parishioners. As soon as they were settled in the car, Irene said, "Ungodly noise, wasn't it?" She was pleased with her pun. Girlie, who had begun the day wishing a plague of boils on Miss Boatwright, wondered at her own powers.

50

"Hello? Hello Out There?"

The congregation was again gathered in knots on the steps of St. Clement's, this time discussing Mrs. Edgar. Only the day before, around three in the afternoon, after drinking a cup of tea and eating a Sao biscuit spread with butter, Mrs. Edgar—they could see her house from where they stood, her husband was a layman at the church—had gone into the garage and hanged herself. She threw a rope over a beam, kicked out the chair. She had cancer, although what kind wasn't specified, out of delicacy. The funeral was on Tuesday.

In the car, Irene pondered Mrs. Edgar's courage. She had been a quiet woman, mousy, given to wearing nylon dresses. "Goes to show," said Irene. Through the back window of the car, Girlie had a view of the garage. She expected it somehow to be transformed by the monstrous event, but it remained resolutely itself: a yellow fibro structure with wooden doors and a corrugated iron roof.

51

Clicky Feet

Serena McGarry was the sort of woman who wore high heels with slacks and her hair in a French twist, so when her husband, Ray, who had been trying to make a go of it on the old Leonard place, shot her and their two young children and then turned the gun on himself, no one was surprised. Boy, who had noticed Serena clicking down the main street of Progress and been rewarded for his attention with a sunny smile, pestered his father for the reason. "Debt," said Rex. End of conversation.

52

Blind as Worms

Nick Pasquale wasn't interested in an affair, not with an unhappy farmer's wife, but he found he liked having Irene around. She began helping him with weddings on Saturday afternoons. Afterwards, they drank beer, played Nana Mouskouri records, and made jokes about the bridal party that had just departed.

As a way of saying thank you, Nick gave her a coral necklace he had bought on his travels—a lovely thing, from Lisbon—but Irene, playing at rectitude, decided that the gift was "inappropriate." She put the necklace in a paper bag and on the next trip to town gave it to Girlie, saying, "Take this to Nick. Tell him I can't keep it."

Girlie walked along the main street of Progress in her box-pleated serge uniform, heavy school shoes, past the post office, the library, the bank.

She stopped at the jeweler's window to examine its array of fountain pens, lockets, identity bracelets, and friendship rings, covetousness rising in her. Catching sight of her reflection in the plate glass—forehead, nose, chin—she straightened her tie, pulled at her beret.

At Fosseys, she eyed a display of mohair wool, flannel nightdresses, and girdles. Seeing the girdles prompted her to say the word "lingerie" under her breath, practicing its pronunciation. For good measure, she followed it with "peignoir," "boutique," and "patio." Heaven forbid she mispronounce these words in her mother's presence.

As she walked, she thought about Irene and Nick, the gift and why it was being returned. She was confused, lost in the woods, the birds eating up the trail of crumbs she was dropping behind her. In the end, she came to only one conclusion: her father was diminished by the transaction.

Nick was at the front desk.

"Here's this. Mum says she can't keep it." She handed him the paper bag, scrunched where she had been holding it.

Nick opened the bag, grunted. Then he went back to ticking off a list of names. Girlie took her cue and left without saying another word.

Once, while waiting for her mother and tiring of examining the photographs that lined the studio walls—it was said that if a girl were pregnant when she married, she was obligated to wear a pink underskirt—Girlie had gone exploring and come across the narrow room where Nick slept.

He had furnished it simply: a single bed, a bureau, and a chair. And he had hung on the wall a reproduction of Vincent van Gogh's painting of his bedroom at Arles, similarly monastic; Nick was a self-conscious man. It was this room of which Girlie thought as she walked back down the main street of Progress to the car where her mother was waiting.

53

Is My Poem a Lion?

Just the person I want to see," said Nick, who was on a ladder fixing a light. Irene and Girlie had just come through the black curtains that separated the studio from the lobby. Girlie assumed that he meant Irene, but it became apparent it was herself when Nick scooted down the ladder and picked up a school magazine lying on a chair. He received a complimentary copy because he took the school photos once a year, lining the students up, class by class, team by team, and saying "cheese" until his jaw ached. Heck of a way to earn a living, as he summed it up.

Nick had marked a page in the school magazine. On the page was a poem by Girlie. It was titled "Grief."

"Good grief, Girlie," he said, wagging the magazine in her face, laughing. When he calmed down, he said, "What do you know about grief? You're only fifteen, for heaven's sakes. Write about what you know!"

This was good advice, but Girlie, afire with shame, couldn't hear him. Nick proceeded to read the poem aloud, with great theatrical flourishes.

Girlie darted at him, grabbed at the magazine.

He held it above her reach and continued to read.

"Stop, Nick," said Irene. "Enough."

54

My Mother Has Grown to an Enormous Height

Girlie was writing an essay on the New Deal when Irene asked her if she wanted to go on an outing to the lake on the other side of Progress. It was Sunday, and Irene was at loose ends. The next day was a big one for her; she had been invited to a garden party at Government House in Canberra to meet the Queen. Freddie had arranged it.

Irene and Girlie set off. Conversation was fitful. Irene remarked on how bad the caterpillars were that year: sacks of them hung from boree trees like grotesque Christmas ornaments. From time to time she slowed down to avoid hitting the galahs that had gathered to eat grain spilled on the verges of the road. In the distance, a thunderstorm quickstepped across the Hay plain.

The route to the lake took them through the

middle of Progress, deserted except for a car doing desultory laps on the main street. The couple in the car were sitting so close they would both fall out if you opened the driver's door.

"Bodgies," said Irene.

Girlie knew the girl in the car. Her name was Christine, and she was a classmate of Girlie's. She was envied for having a steady boyfriend.

"She'll be married at eighteen, a hag by the time she's thirty," continued Irene. "Don't let it happen to you." Privately, she believed that the likelihood of Girlie—shy, gawky, homely Girlie—marrying early was low, but a warning never hurt. Boy was another matter.

Girlie glanced across at her mother and noticed that Irene was wearing the coral necklace. She turned away, studied the war memorial. Irene caught the look, saw her daughter's face grow puffy with suppressed emotion, and thought, not for the first time, what a starchy little miss her daughter was. And so unforgiving.

At the lake, they parked and wound down the windows, letting in air that smelled of exhaust from speedboats. The lake, dirty green in color, was artificial, filled with run-off water from the farms. The town council had installed picnic benches on its foreshores; saplings guarded with netting struggled to survive. Cumbungi grew just under the surface of the lake, a forest of it, thick and slimy. Weed was forever fouling the propellers of boats, and if you fell off your skis, it grabbed at your legs. Still, there wasn't another stretch of recreational water within a hundred miles.

As they watched, a swan glided from the bulrushes, splashed into the air, swooped on a water-skier. At first Irene and Girlie thought it was attacking the skier; swans are territorial, quarrelsome. The skier must have thought so, too, because she put up an arm to shield her face. But that wasn't the case; the swan was flying next to the skier, keeping her company. They did several laps together before the swan tired of the game and returned to the bulrushes.

Irene told Girlie about some dolphins she had seen catching waves at the beach. "For the sheer hell of it," she said. She turned to Girlie, her face lit with enthusiasm. Had Girlie ever seen crows playing? Lined up on a fence, swinging from it? She mimed their movements. Girlie hadn't.

They were only a mile away from home, passing through an intersection, when a utility driven by a workman from a nearby farm clipped the back mudguard of their car and caused it to become airborne. Girlie saw black, felt a rushing of wind. When she opened her eyes, she was still in her seat, but the car was balanced on the shoulder of a drainage ditch. She pushed at the door, scrambled down.

Irene was lying under the car, her head and torso protruding. She was unconscious, covered with blood and dust. The vehicle that had hit them was turned around in the road, facing the direction from which it had come. Its driver had a gash on his forehead; blood veiled his face. He stayed where he was and wailed.

Girlie walked in small circles in the middle of the road. Someone must have heard the collision. Then, unable to bear doing nothing, she dragged Irene from under the car. She squatted next to her mother, clearing clods of earth from under her head, making soothing noises, instructing her to wake up, tomorrow she had to meet the Queen.

The sun was setting. The injured man kept up his wailing, a thin, high sound such as a whistling kettle makes. Girlie was annoyed by it. Then she noticed that the coral necklace was biting into her mother's throat. She attempted to loosen the necklace by undoing the catch. It wouldn't budge. In her panic, she tugged at the necklace, pulling, twisting. At that moment, blood bubbled from her mother's mouth, purple, not red, or so it seemed in the inky light.

An idea detonated in Girlie's mind: she had killed her mother, choked her. Girlie's hands fell to her sides.

55

Dawn Comes Slowly
and Changes Nothing

Irene was in the hospital for three months. Whenever Girlie visited, her mother found fault, saying, "Get your hair out of your eyes," or "Straighten your shoulders." Girlie said nothing. Instead, she fingered the edge of the coverlet on the bed and took deep breaths of air cut with disinfectant.

Rex didn't fare any better. He would bring her whatever she had requested—books, magazines, chocolate biscuits, flowers from the garden—and then drift off to other patients to talk crops and the weather.

Boy stayed away from the hospital. He was preoccupied. He had a steady girlfriend, and they were "doing it" at every opportunity.

56

Commonsense Cookery

Irene came home on crutches. Rex had prepared a nourishing soup for her in a large iron pot.

"Delicious," she said.

The second time he served it, she asked what it was.

"Sheep's head soup," he told her. His mother had made it in the Depression years. The recipe was simple: a sheep's head, carrots and onions or whatever was at hand, seasoning, simmer for several days. The head had to be cleaned thoroughly, of course.

Irene fumbled for her crutches, jerked across the kitchen to the stove, where she jabbed at the contents of the pot with a fork. The head hadn't yet boiled to a skull; it had ears, skin, tufts of wool.

Irene's eyes swiveled, mad and enflamed.

57

My Secret Love

Irene had inherited at least one of her father's prejudices. She was always sounding off about the Catholic church, its large families, scheming clergy. Whenever they saw a church on a hill, Irene predicted it would be Catholic. She and the children then looked for the tell-tale signs of Catholicism—heavy wrought-iron door hinges, bricks the color of liver, an institutional air—and invariably found them. Just as invariably, Irene would remark, "Trust the Micks to grab the highest spot."

With this kind of practice, Girlie knew right away when Graham Trethewey joined her class that he was Catholic. Graham was a fleshy, downy, handsome boy, seventeen years old, ripe as a peach. He had been expelled from Riverview College in Sydney for taking a skiff and stealing provisions—booze, mainly—from pleasure boats. His parents had sent him to Girlie's school to sit for the Leaving Certificate.

Graham—Catholic, bad—exerted the same pull on Girlie as her mother's books. And Graham quite liked Girlie. Actually, he didn't differentiate among females: he was magnanimous in that respect. Plain or beautiful, smart or dumb, they were all potential conquests to him. If they didn't oblige, he moved on, no hurt feelings.

Graham discovered Girlie had access to her mother's car, and they started going to movies together. Driving home, Graham would turn up the radio, take Girlie's hand, place it on his crotch. Kathy Kirby was filling the airwaves that year, shouting about love and daffodils. Girlie didn't want to displease him, so she sat there, sweaty, rigid, her arm and eardrums aching, enjoying none of it.

One weekend they went to the river. Graham led Girlie along the bank, solicitously holding back branches to ease her passage. When they had gone a distance, Graham took a towel from the canvas satchel he was carrying and laid it on the ground, then gave Girlie a long, imploring look. Take pity on me! he signaled. His eyes traveled to the towel, in case she hadn't caught his meaning. Girlie turned on her heel, backtracking through the scrub to the car, not waiting for Graham to catch up. She thought she would like to plunge into the river, into the opaque green water, and swim without stopping, swim forever.

58

Dipping His Wick

Boy's girlfriend, April, was pregnant. Boy was out of his mind with worry. He lay awake at night, sobbing. He was seventeen, and his life was over. He would have to marry, stay on the farm. Bawling kids, dirty nappies, fly-blown sheep, bone-shaking tractors, hot sun. All his mother's warnings came back to him.

His girlfriend, who wanted to be a school-teacher, was as horrified as he was. They put their heads together, plotted. She obtained the address of a doctor in Sydney from a knowledgeable cousin; he used his savings to buy tickets for the plane that went daily to the city. On the appointed day, instead of going to school, the couple hitch-hiked to the airport.

To their embarrassment, the airline hostess was a girl they knew; she had left school only the year before. When she came around with sandwiches on little plastic trays, April pressed her face up against the window and exclaimed over the patchwork of paddocks, managing to forestall questions about the purpose of their trip.

April, understandably, wasn't hungry. Boy unwrapped the cellophane and ate both sandwiches: ham, cheese, gherkin, layered between thin slices of white bread. The sandwiches came with a cocktail onion apiece, and he popped those in his mouth as well.

Stiff-legged, they caught a taxi to the doctor's office, where the deed was done. April cried all the way home. She made no sound, but tears slipped down her face. Boy tried to comfort her, making jokes about her red nose. He was feeling as if he had been released from prison.

Outside the plane, clouds had collected in disorderly heaps: wool waiting to be sorted, graded, baled.

59

Thieves in the Night

First Girlie went, then Boy, into the world. As a leave-taking present, Irene sewed Girlie a low-cut, lolly-pink ballgown and then took her shopping at Fosseys for a push-up brassiere. When it was Boy's turn, Irene and Boy stayed up late singing at the piano, finishing with "Goodnight, Sweetheart."

60

Burning Silence

Rex and Irene had given up arguing. He no longer bothered to tell her that he wasn't asking much—harvest his crops, care for his animals, share it all with a good woman, tra-la—and Irene didn't reply that far from not asking much, he was asking everything.

Rex went about his work, unchaining his dogs at first light, going from paddock to paddock to check on the livestock, tipping bales of hay from the tailboard of his utility, and then crouching in its lee to drink tea from a thermos flask and watch the sheep converge on the feed. They came running, bouncing, vaulting, on short legs.

Irene did whatever she pleased, sometimes returning home quite late in the evening.

61

Goodbye to the Farm

Irene walked out on Rex on a hot day in early January. Rex was in the kitchen eating his lunch—lamb-shank stew, plum pudding and custard, the plum pudding left over from Christmas—when she came in, dressed to go to town, carrying the larger of the family's two suitcases. She turned toward him, her face blank.

The dogs were asleep on the verandah, twitching in the heat, groaning in the backs of their throats. Irene said nothing, blinked as if drugged, kicked the screen door open, exited. Rex thought, almost idly, about running after her, pleading with her to stay. He thought about picking up his shotgun, shooting her, turning the gun on himself. He stayed where he was, in his seat.

He heard her car cough into life, putter past the meathouse, the petrol tank, the shearers' quarters.

He went out to the garden to watch her progress. The car disappeared behind the clump of black box trees. Minutes later it reappeared on the road that led straight to the front gate. Irene slowed down for the ramp, bumped across it, made the right hand turn onto the main road.

The view from where Rex stood was panoramic: an immense blue sky, green rice fields, shimmering heat. The car traversed his entire field of vision; he moved his eyes, tracking it. Finally, the car vanished behind the stand of boxes at the far corner of the property, materialized on the other side, was on the bridge, was gone.

62

Oh Hold Me, for I Am Afraid

For the next week, Rex was a man out of his skin. He couldn't eat or sleep or sit still. He walked. He walked the circumference of the farm, clockwise and then anticlockwise. He crisscrossed it, bisecting the paddocks one day, following the fence line the next. He walked all day and through the night. Sometimes it seemed to him as if there were no sound; he was under water. At other times, his hearing was hypersensitive, and he picked up every scrape, scurry, murmur. It was a week leading to a full moon, and his nighttime wanderings were bathed in phosphorescence.

After five days of no sleep and no food, he decided that God was walking with him. He was mildly surprised, never before having experienced even the slightest stirring of religious feeling, but he accepted it without question and rather enjoyed the company. On the seventh day, he found himself alone again. That night he slept, and when he woke his hair had turned white. But he was no longer numb; he was angry. He was a volcano of anger.

Irene had left almost everything behind: clothes, books, magazines, records, photographs, some crested china that had belonged to her mother, a silver cruet, a wooden Buddha brought back from China by an adventurous great-uncle. Rex threw it all into the incinerator, where it made a merry fire. The records congealed into a black lump: *Carousel, Kismet, The Pajama Game, Harry Belafonte at Carnegie Hall, Liszt Piano Concertos* became one.

Next, in a gesture of symbolic spite, he bought two hundred pigs. They were not prize pigs. They were runty and unappealing, with long skinny bodies and splotchy pinkish-white skin and shifty pink-rimmed eyes. Rex thought they were unique.

To shelter the pigs, he acquired six corrugated-iron water tanks, cut them in half, and laid them in rows. The paddock where he did this took on the aspect of a World War II army barracks. He also purchased a quantity of tractor tires and cut them in half, and into the halves he put spoiled vegetables, which he would fetch from the market gardens in his utility.

He opened up every gate on the farm, and the pigs mapped the farm as thoroughly as he had done, but with their snouts. He also left open the gate to the yard of the house, and soon none of Irene's garden was left. They rooted up the irises and the cannas, pulled down the passion-fruit vine, demolished the red-hot poker, sheared the shrubs—the broom, the bottlebrush, the crepe myrtle, the Chinese lantern—to nubs. The only plants left standing were oleanders; even pigs can't digest their leaves.

He sold them a month later for a tidy profit. Never a big drinker, he started going to the pub in the evening. He liked best to talk about pigs. "If a man lay down to sleep and pigs came along, there would be nothing left of him but his shoelaces," he would say admiringly while tracing a pattern in a puddle of beer with an index finger.

He would sit at the bar until closing time and seem perfectly sober, if a little careful, until he stood up to leave, when he would list alarmingly and have to be helped. One time he got off his bar stool and fell over, poleaxed, face down on the floor, amongst the cigarette stubs and discarded betting tickets.

63

Heavy Stones and Hard Lines

Six months to the day after Irene left, Rex drove his car into the Murrumbidgee River, which was in the early stages of flooding. The water was muddy, swift, visibly rising. He went to a bluff he knew from a duck-shooting expedition, down a rutted track near a sawmill, and pressed the accelerator flat. Twenty-four hours later, and the water would have been too high; it would have broken its banks, spilling into paddocks like a woman in evening dress settling her skirts.

The car sank slowly and lopsidedly, the passenger side becoming immersed first. If there had been anyone watching, they would have seen Rex sitting in the driver's seat, as erect as could be in the circumstance, holding onto the steering wheel, staring ahead, the brown water up to his chest, his shoulders, his chin.

The car became caught in the burly current. By this time, only the roof and a few inches of window were visible, and if one looked very closely, the top of Rex's head, for he was still clinging determinedly to the wheel, as if this were a mad carnival ride. The car corkscrewed three times and disappeared.

He left no note for Girlie and Boy. For years he had felt that they were passengers on a train going God knows where, and he was a solitary figure by the railway line, waving, at first cordially, but then like a man possessed, until he was waving at nothing. Writing a note to them would be the same as addressing the blurred faces on just such a passing train. Faces that never gained definition no matter how hard he stared. For one thing, the train was going too fast. For another, the sun was shining low in the afternoon sky, its rays glancing off the glass of the windows.

PART FOUR

1

The New Life I Demand of My Bones

The day you left Rex, your hands were trembling. To calm yourself, you adjusted the side window of the car so that air streamed over your face, parting your hair, flattening it against your skull. Next, you recited species of wattle tree: *Acacia baileyana, Acacia decurrens, Acacia longifolia, Acacia pycnantha, Acacia saligna* . . . You pictured each one: blossoms, foliage, bark. Thus steadied, you began to sing. You always sang when you were alone in a car. Broadway show tunes.

2

Oh, I Could Live with Thee in the Wildwood

You didn't strike out on your own. You were intelligent, curious, energetic, but you needed a man, or so you thought. It wasn't Freddie. He had become a politician as he planned. The Honorable Frederick Garlick. Nor was it Nick. He had returned to Sydney, summoned by his mother. No, it was someone new, and, following the migratory pattern of Australian adulterers, the two of you went north, to monsoons and mangrove swamps, water buffalo and brolgas, whip snakes and crocodiles.

3

Idiocy Is the Female Defect

Are you happy? On and off. Inside you, dissatisfaction still caws like a crow. You like to quote Hippocrates: "Life is short, the occasion fleeting, experience deceitful, and judgment difficult." The literary figure with whom you most identify is Oscar Wilde. You keep *De Profundis* beside your bed. As unlikely as the parallel might seem—witty fop, farmer's wife—you feel as he did: pilloried by the ungenerous, exiled.

Increasingly, you express bewilderment at the direction your life has taken. None of it adds up. When your son comes north to visit, you always ask, "Darling Boy, where did the years go?" Your voice isn't plaintive, as might be expected, but querulous and accusing, as if you had no part in it, as if someone stole the years from under your nose.

ABOUT THE AUTHOR

Kate Jennings grew up on a farm near Griffith, New South Wales, and in the 1960s attended Sydney University. Her books include two volumes of poems, *Come to Me My Melancholy Baby* (1975) and *Cats, Dogs & Pitchforks* (1993); two books of essays, *Save Me, Joe Louis* (1989) and *Bad Manners* (1993); and a collection of stories, *Women Falling Down in the Streets* (1990). She also edited *Mother I'm Rooted,* an anthology of poetry by women. *Snake* is her first novel and the first of her books to be published in the United States. Since 1979 Jennings has lived in New York City.